FEAR(LESS)

Amos Ethan Laar

To order additional copies of this book, contact:
Xlibris
844-714-8691
www.Xlibris.com
Orders@Xlibris.com

ISBN: Softcover   978-1-6698-5016-8
           EBook   978-1-6698-5017-5

Print information available on the last page

Rev. date: 10/17/2022

Inspiration

Inspired by books I read, and movies I watched during lockdown (August 2020 to April 2021). The boredom of being at home all day, all week throughout the year pushed me to write this book. I got further inspiration from my Dad (Professor Amos Laar) who always pushed me to work harder and harder. His pep talks inspired me to finish the book after I showed him the first draft.

Acknowledgements

I would like to acknowledge some very special people who made very special contributions to this book. First, I extend sincere thanks to my 6th Grade School Teacher Mr. Michael Rossi (of Michael Rossi - Thomas Street Middle School, Mississauga, Canada). Mr. Michael Rossi encouraged and motivated me and my classmates to read for a minimum of 40 minutes everyday. With this guidance, and given that we were all 'locked down' due to the COVID pandemic, I read about four (4) books every week. It was during this time that I got to grow my writing style, my imagination and some of my many ideas to write this book. I also want to acknowledge Mr. Bright Aweh, and Ms. Patience Ablor (both of St. Albans International School, Accra, Ghana). They were very supportive during my formative years when I spent eight years at this School. Mr. Marko Jurisic (my 7th Grade School Teacher, St Joseph Catholic Elementary School, Cambridge, ON, Canada). Mr. Jurisic has also being very supportive. And my parents (Prof. Amos Laar, and Dr. Matilda Laar) who never stopped believing in me, who helped me, and guided me along the way as I wrote this book. I thank Mr. Silver Nanema (of House of Mentoring and Research Resources, Accra, Ghana) for helping me with the infographics, and my Auntie (Elfrieda Montford) for proofreading the final version of the manuscript. I would also like to thank Ms. Celestine Nudanu of Nexus Editing Services, Accra for proofreading the initial draft of the manuscript. Finally, I cannot thank Dr. Ireneous Soyiri (Uncle Soyiri) enough for his continued guidance and support. He inspires me a lot.

Dedication

To all children wherever they are.

CHAPTER ONE: THE JOURNEY BEGINS

A million years ago, when the continents of the world were connected, there was a god called Oya. He was known for his control of storms, lightning and wind. This god is an orisha of winds, lightning, violent storms, death and rebirth. Oya came to earth to look for his bride. He met Maisha, and he married. Maisha's son married a woman called Martha. In time, they had children, and their children grew up and gave Maisha a great grand-son called Chaltas.

As a child Chaltas received a magical flute from his uncle. The flute was passed on to his uncle, but his uncle found no use for it. Unbeknownst to him it was magical as it was enchanted by the dying breath of Oya. Chaltas had an older sibling called Zach. One day Zach wandered into a distant kingdom that no one had heard of. This kingdom was much more powerful than theirs. Thrilled by his discovery, he quickly returned to his village and told them about this new kingdom, but nobody would believe him not even his parents. Indeed, it was an abomination to talk about unknown kingdoms. Zach was banished from his kingdom for persistently telling this story. His only choice was to return to this kingdom and accepted when its King (the Ice Kingdom) noticed his knowledge of herbal remedies. During his stay, the King appointed him to be the wizard's apprentice. Zack learned and practised magic from the wizards. Eventually, he became the chief wizard and was in charge of protecting the kingdom. By doing so, he summoned an ice golem. The ice golem ensured no one could enter. Although he had confidence in the golems, he knew the ultimate power to protect any kingdom is contained in Chaltas' flute. This is something he discovered after training in the art of spells and chants. One night, he sent one of his messengers to capture Chaltas' mom from his old village, so as to lure Chaltas into this new kingdom. He asked the messengers to leave a note for Chaltas.

Chaltas loved to play his flute. His father was a merchant and often embarked on long trips to ply his trade. His mother worked three days a week. She was a baker; she owned one of the most popular bakeries in the village. With his parents out most of the time, Chaltas often invited his best friend Tau over to play. Their favourite sport was riding bulls. The fierce animals were not easy to ride. Therefore, every time they rode one for a couple of minutes, Chaltas's mom would reward them with special treats from the bakery.

Tau was one of Chaltas's best friends because of how much they had in common. Tau was originally from a Viking city. He and his parents fled and came to settle in Chaltas village. Chaltas and Tau both had an item with extraordinary magical powers. Chaltas had a flute and Tau, a spear. Interestingly, they were not aware of the magical attributes of their items. In Tau's parents' words, the spear is just for protection, and he is to take it everywhere he goes.

Tau's parents stole the spear and incited chaos. The warrior with a spear was the only man protecting the city. Tau's grandfather was one of the warriors who could wield the spear and when he died it was going to be passed on to another person. That other person wasn't Tau so his parents bolted with the spear.

CHAPTER 2: THE FLUTE

One day when Chaltas was playing his flute, items in his room started to float. As soon as he stopped playing the flute, the floating items fell with a thud. He was left spell-bound, with his jaw dropping in amazement. Whenever he used the flute to move things in his room and stopped, the crashing noise that the floating items made, when they came tumbling down, was a matter of concern to his parents.

"What's all that noise, Chaltas?" His parents would ask

"Nothing." Chaltas would respond

One morning, when Chaltas' mother had left the house for work, he saw a strange note on his mom's bed. Curious, Chaltas picked up the note and read it.

> Beware! Monsters made of ice, stone and fire lurk in the dark. To get your mom, you must defeat these golems - moss, ice and fire. To do so, you must journey to three kingdoms; the first is the moss, the second is fire, and the third is ice.

The words were glowing; he knew it was not from his kingdom. His village never allowed magic ink. He read in the books that glowing items must be magic. He had questions about his flute. Was it an illusion? He asked himself. He was extremely terrified because of the coat of magic ink. He quickly rushed out of his house to go and get Tau to come and see it. "My parents wouldn't allow me to go outside the kingdom, let alone fight monsters made of ice, moss, and fire" he muttered to himself. Despite knowing only one of its powers, he grabbed his flute and left. Tau was

sharpening his spear when Chaltas arrived at his house.

"Tau will you come with me?" Chaltas asked.

Chaltas showed him the note. Tau agreed to follow him to help him find his mom. Tau took his spear

and followed Chaltas. Tau told Chaltas along the way that they needed more help, such as a team. They

were not exactly strong plus they had no idea how to be warriors. So, they went to Master Ou, the

wizard of the Kingdom, but he was not there. They met a boy in the cloak, who was Master Ou's son.

"My father no longer practices as a wizard, he has resigned," he said. He told them his name was Ou.

And they showed him the note. A girl who was on her way to the fletcher, overheard them talking and

asked if she could come along with them. Chaltas could not say no because of two things. First, he was

astonished by her beauty. Second, he needed all the help he could get. The girl's name was Lexi. Chaltas

looked at his map that showed the whole surrounding area and the three kingdoms. He walked in the

direction that would lead him to the Moss Kingdom. The journey had begun.

They were travelling in the general direction of the Moss Kingdom until it got dark. They looked for shelter. Chaltas and Lexi went to look for sticks. They gathered sticks and made a shelter and slept peacefully. When he woke up Lexi was making some arrows out of the spare sticks. Chaltas wanted to show the flute to Ou, so he started playing, but this time the things around him did not float, instead he and his "team" started floating. Ou was stunned. He had seen the flute before in one of his father's books, he asked Chaltas how he got it and Chaltas said his uncle gave it to him as a present.

"Can you play your flute again" Ou asked. Chaltas played the flute, but this time nothing happened. Tau saw some people approaching them quickly. Chaltas also saw a couple of weird stone figures just before he was knocked out.

9

CHAPTER 3: THE BATTLES BEGIN

Suddenly, they were captured by the Queen's guards and taken into a fighting arena. Chaltas checked his map and he was right on track for the first golem. The Queen of the Moss kingdom came out and announced that they were to fight some of her champions. They had a couple of days to prepare. Ou marched towards the centre of the village arena and quickly inspected it. He scoped the terrain. It was rocky and full of slippery moss. Chaltas, Tau, and Lexi, on the other hand, were exploring the markets. The sights were stunning; every corner was green with lush vegetation.

"This place is gorgeous take away the fact that we are captured," Chaltas said.

Chaltas bought a sword from the market. The seller told him it was one of the highest quality.

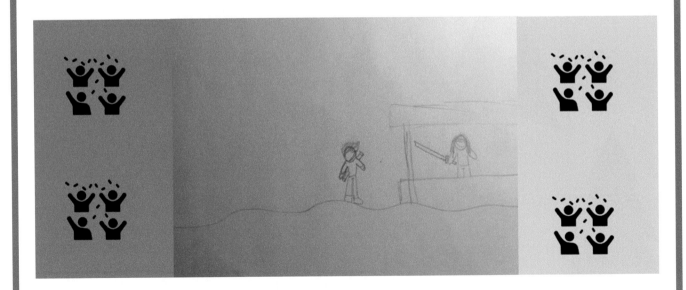

Chaltas blurted out only to see everyone looking at him giggling. "Every weapon is the finest weapon when it comes to these Merchants, said Lexi. They collected a few weapons, grabbed a meal and slept to regain their strength for the battle. The day of the battle was here. Over the span of three days, they had to battle a barbarian, a caveman and finally the grass golem.

They huddled up in a circle and the barbarian was unleashed. Ou saw guards escorting the contestants out of the arena. He lunged at them and the team split up leaving Lexi. Lexi rolled under the barbarian's legs and shot an arrow at his back. Ou thrusted his ancient staff and out came lightning that stunned the barbarian.

"Did the lightning come out of your staff?" Tau asked.

"Yes, but focus on the battle," Ou shouted.

Chaltas played his flute and the mystical flute gifted him a sword. He had training using a sword; it was part of his basic defence training, so he quickly tucked his flute away and joined the battle. He slashed the barbarian but his sword broke.

"One of the finest quality?" Lexi said with a grin. Only the lightning from Ou's staff affected the barbarian. His sword slowly reformed. "It is the best in the world, it reforms!" screamed Chaltas. He played his flute again and immediately he was surrounded by flames. He ran faster, then bolted and slashed the barbarian.

Tau threw his spear and impaled the barbarian. Lexi shot some arrows that pinned him down and, Ou

blasted a ball of fire which fell on his chest. Chaltas sliced again with his sword. The barbarian had fallen, only a few warriors had ever beaten the barbarian. They had done it! Tau, Chaltas and Ou stayed around to see the damage the had caused to the terrain. All the lush greenery in the arena was gone and there was dust everywhere pieces of rock lay on the ground. The group moved deeper into the kingdom and they set up a camp there. As Ou was getting ready to rest, he noticed something about all of them in the battle, specifically their strengths and weaknesses. Lexi: Lexi liked to do things on her own, but she was a very good archer. Chaltas had amazing powers but no idea how to use them and Tau's spear was no ordinary weapon, but Tau can't control it. Ou slept with this in his mind someone needed to help them get through their weaknesses and heighten their abilities.

The next day they had to fight the **caveman**, so they were discussing tactics that will help them win. The caveman was furious. He smashed through the arena walls with his club, he knocked Ou into the crowd of people. Ou flew back, his staff was broken. Tau tried to smash the caveman with his spear, but the caveman bashed him first. Lexi shot a couple of arrows at the caveman, but they just broke. The caveman bashed onto the ground, and all of them flew into the sky. Chaltas got out his flute whilst he was falling down and started playing then, a massive hand came out from the flute and it caught them. Then he realized that the hand did everything he did. The hand punched then punched the caveman, but the caveman blocked with his club. The magical hand faded away. He played the flute for some time now. The flute was charging up its power and then out of the flute came the hand again and Chaltas's arm was surrounded in flames. Chaltas got a flaming right hand, a massive mystical hand precisely been controlled by his left. They all attacked the caveman, arrows by Lexi, Ou blasted a ball of flame, and the spear came bashing down from Tau's hand. The arrows shot by Lexi had flames on them; a fist of flame from Chaltas on the caveman's face e and he was finished. The day had ended; everyone injured.

Tomorrow, they fight the **grass golem**, which was according to the note, the stone. Ou explained to Chaltas as he studied the flute that specific notes is the key to unlocking different powers. Ou got a piece of paper and started to jot down notes that give Chaltas certain powers. Ou stopped and rested as all of his friends were asleep.

 During the night, Chaltas had a nightmare, He dreamt that his friends had died, his flute was broken, and the Moss golemhad killed his mother. He immediately got up and started playing his flute to calm down and with the intention of trying to unlock the powers he had not used before. He played the flute until Lexi woke up. She noticed he was disturbed. "Chaltas, what's up, you look as if you've seen a ghost."

Chaltas narrated his nightmare to Lexi, who took his hand played a song from a musical paper that she gave him. As he played a lion suddenly appeared from the flute, first it was just dust floating in the air, which then transformed into a lion. Chaltas exclaimed: I didn't know my flute could conjure a lion with the right notes. He sat on the lion and was armoured up in fine chainmail that also came from the dust. Lexi gave him a nudge, and she said we will be fine just give some of the flute power on my arrows. They both laughed.

CHAPTER 4 FINISHING

When the friends woke up, they stepped out and there were posters everywhere.

<u>Battle of the century</u>
Chaltas Lexi Ou and Tau

vs

Moss golem

<u>Battle of the century</u>
Chaltas Lexi Ou and Tau

vs

Moss golem

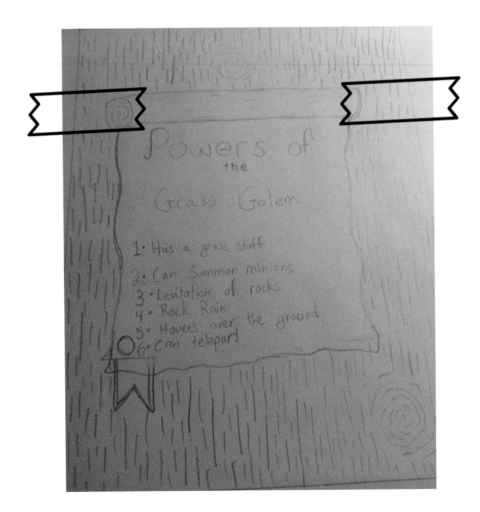

As they entered the arena, they saw another poster that read.

So, the battle began, the arena was full. People were fighting over seats. People made banners of the moss golem they had seen him fight once but it lasted for just a few seconds. Ou explained something to them about the rock rain the rocks were made of hard diamond and the fire around them was hotter than a furnace as Chaltas, Lexi, Ou and Tau walked into the fighting arena, the crowd erupted. Then the Moss golem teleported into the arena and lunged straight onto Ou. Ou ducked, Lexi took out her arrows, and Tau took out his spear, and Chaltas played his flute using the same notes that were on the sheet that Lexi had given to him. The flaming armoured lion then emerged and Chaltas' rode the lion past Lexi's arrows, making them glow. As Tau was about to bash the golem, the lion passed by his spear and now there was a mystical glow on the spear, making it bigger. Lexi's bow turned into a crossbow, and she started floating. Ou's staff was fixed and it summoned up a beast. Ou controlled the beast. The lion roared and the golem flew out of control, but he hovered back, summoning some golem minions. The golem minions were much bigger than the four. They towered over Chaltas and his friends and tried to smash them, but Tau's spear blocked them. Tau jumped and smashed into one of the minions faces. The monster cut one of the minions' legs and it tumbled down. Chaltas brought out a flaming sword and Lexi shot five arrows at a minion with her crossbow. Chaltas went after the Moss golem. He run and slashed but the golem teleported behind him and punched him down, but he got up again and pierced the sword to the ground and made flames all around the golem. The golem blasted a ball of rock rain. Chaltas rolled away, his friends had finished defeating the minions. The Golem raised up some boulders that were lying around the arena and smashed it onto Tau. Tau could not react because he did not see the boulder. Tau was taken out of the arena. He was seriously injured. Then Chaltas was raging. He took Tau's spear in his other hand and pierced the golem then slashed with his sword off the golem's arms, but the golem did not go down easily. He had one last card. He brought out the staff of the jungle, which allowed him to turn into any jungle animal. He turned into a snake and slithered past Chaltas, then he turned into a tiger and slashed the back of Chaltas. Chaltas

15

fell and Lexi rushed behind him and saw the blood. She quickly called the guards to take him out of the arena. Chaltas did not want to go, he wanted to finish the battle, so they allowed him. This time he did not play the flute, but he was on fire, he run at the speed of lightning and slashed and jumped. The spectators could not see him because he ran so fast and red-hot sparks came out of his sword as he ran. He finally stopped, and the golem tumbled and fell. Chaltas was taken out of the arena; he was no longer bleeding. Some of the power from the flute had entered Chaltas's body and stopped the bleeding. Chaltas and his friends went to see if Tau was ok. Tau was fine, and he just needed to rest. After Tau was fully rested the Queen let them get out of the village because they had defeated her champions. He took the flute and continued his quest for his mother. They traded pieces of the rock golem's minions for some food, a map, healing remedies and a bestiary. What is the bestiary for? Tau asked. To keep record of the monsters we come across and their powers and weaknesses so if we encounter them again, we know how to defeat them, Ou replied.

THE BESTIARY (Ou did a bit of designing the front cover)

They camped out for the night and Tau and Chaltas made a large roasted turkey that they had gotten for trading for the pieces of the minions, and Ou drew the golem into the bestiary and described his powers. Ou also got some of the minion pieces and as he examined Tau's spear the rock entered the spear. It set off a bright light and all the others looked at it the spear was now new and improved. Ou said he would have new powers so Tau could not wait to use it. They set off again in the direction that will take them towards the Ice kingdom and they broke some wood with Tau's spear and Lexi used some of the branches to make arrows and they made a shelter out of some vines leaves and wood.

CHAPTER 5: SAVAGE SCAVENGERS

They set off, next on the map was the Forbidden Pyramid.

After days of travelling, they finally reached the desert in search of the Pyramid, but they were approached by scavengers. Scavengers were these small people thateat whatever food they have access to. They are very hostile; they hate it when people enter their territory. Chaltas's flame hand slashed three of the Scavengers in half, Lexi shot arrows at two of them, Ou shot three flame balls at five of them, but it was not enough so he split them into eight smaller balls and destroyed most of them. As Tau was about to tackle the last scavenger, the **scavenger** blurted: wait, wait, wait, you've come for the Pyramid? How did you know that? asked Chaltas. Who comes into the desert for anything other than the Pyramid? The scavenger answered.

"I will help you; I know where in the Pyramid their weapons are,"

So, the scavenger joined them on their quest. They had reached the Pyramid and mobs of scavengers started chasing them. They all attacked. Chaltas punched five with a huge magic hand. Lexi shot arrows with her cross bow at four scavengers.

Tau knocked into eight scavengers, Ou threw his staff and missed all the scavengers the first time, then it flew back with speed and sliced three of them. **Suddenly giant spiders** assaulted them from the nearby caves. One bit Lexi and poisoned her, luckily for Lexi the poison only weakens, it doesn't kill. Chaltas sliced spider after spider. Ou blasted lightning

18

balls at several spiders. Tau summoned a horse with his magical spear and rode over four spiders, crushing them.

They had defeated the spiders. Lexi and the scavenger were on the ground where the spider had bitten their arms and they were poisoned, they had to make a shelter that could last for a few days for Lexi to get healed. So, they went to find building materials. Ou needed some magical herbs to cure the weakness. So, Ou went to get some from the supply bag. Lexi and the scavenger were poisoned so they needed two of the magical herbs. Chaltas put a cast on Lexi's arm to support it. They needed a shelter but there were dangerous mobs of scavengers and spiders outside and, in the Pyramid. They still needed shelter they started building while Chaltas kept the mob of scavengers at bay by waving his massive hand at them. They had built a small hut for now; they went inside and while the others were asleep Lexi and Chaltas were still awake. Chaltas asked Lexi why she joined them. She said,

"I also travel with my family, but this time my parent left me behind. The trips are boring. We only get to stay in while they trade. I wanted an adventure, a real adventure."

Lexi removed the cast and tried to use her crossbow her hand could not stand to hold the weight of the crossbow. Chaltas held the crossbow for her, but she could not fight the mobs let alone the ice and flame golems. They practiced throughout the night and went to bed and Lexi thanked Chaltas for helping her. "It is the least I could do" Chaltas said The next morning Chaltas went to get some food and supplies. He had enough of the rocks they got from defeating the moss golem. Such rocks are valuable as the could be barter-traded for food and other supplies.

In search of food, Chaltas journeyed to a nearby village. The Chief of that village had heard rumours about him fight, so he pleaded to let him protect their village for a day and he will give him everything in the stalls. Chaltas was so excited. He ran back and alerted his friends and told them to expand the hut, but it was dangerous, another person could get poisoned by the spiders, and Ou did not have any more herbs. They needed the supplies, and if they did not have shelter the mobs would get them. They agreed and went to the village. Lexi had her crossbow strapped around her injured left hand and she would use her other hand to shoot the arrows. They travelled to the village. As before, Tau assembled his **mystical horses** with his improved spear So, they journeyed on the horses. Chaltas played his flute and got some cool looking armour. That he took out of the supply bag Lexi got a chain plate, trousers and boots, she wore it. Chaltas got an iron chest plate and the boots and denims were the same as the chest plate. Lexi saw at a distance a large building with bull cages surrounding them.

Tau summoned up his own armour emerald trouser with a helmet. Ou got something quite different it was a cloak he wore it on top of his old one and suddenly turned invisible. He asked the others how he looked (which was funny because they could not see him).

He heard them laughing and he took it off. They got to the village as weird men on massive bulls started chasing the villagers, who all entered their huts. They had gotten here thinking they would have time to set up defenses.

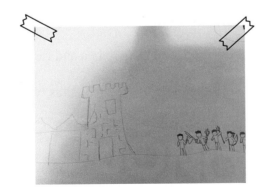

CHAPTER 6: VINDICATED VILLAGE

Another battle started as soon as all the villagers went into their little huts. The scavengers looked at the team, and Lexi drew an arrow from her back, Chaltas's flame hand was ignited, and he had a sword in his other hand, Tau had his spear in his hand, and Ou wore his new cloak. They had to protect the village. Chaltas lunged at one scavenger, but it dodged and tried to slash at him. He played his flute, and the mystical lion came to help. These scavengers had swords bows, and explosives. Lexi shot arrows randomly because she could not see who to focus on. Chaltas and the lion attacked. The lion took on a a group of scavengers as Chaltas went after one of them. Chaltas's flame hand sliced through the scavenger like it was nothing, the lion slashed at the group, the scavenger threw an explosive at one of the huts, and it exploded leaving massive damage on the village. Ou pushed his staff into the dirt and vines grew and most of them got entangled. It was Lexi's chance to attack she shot 10 arrows at the at the entangled scavengers and six of them landed. Tau threw his spear and impaled three of them. The scavengers are coming from the ruins. Said Lexi. We must protect the village. Said Chaltas. Then I will go alone, shouted Lexi, as she run toward the ruins. Lexi saw there were more scavengers. She snuck and saw they were now getting their weapons. In the middle of the ruins she saw stacks of dynamites. She got the two pieces of rubble and ignited the dynamite. Meanwhile her team was still protecting the village. Tau threw his spear toward the large mob of scavengers approaching Chaltas. Chaltas thanked

Tau as Ou kept on hold the scavengers off. When they found Lexi, they informed her that it was time to go inside one of the village huts. Chaltas went to the village Chief that promised him food and supplies. The Chief thanked him profusely.

The villagers agreed that they should be thrown a **feast**. He went look for the rest of his team who agreed to attend the feast. They sat at the large table and ate. Then Tau gathered horses as Chaltas and Lexi built a carriage out of some of materials the village had offered them. They used the carriage to travel back to the desert base, but they had a stowaway in the back It was a wolf. They only noticed it right after they got "home." Chaltas and Ou used mystical powers to lift rocks and other heavy things to fortify the base and Tau put them in place. Lexi however was stroking the wolf and gave it bones from the animals they hunted. She later told the team that the wolf was not willing to go back in to the woods; he wanted to stay with them. They all agreed to keep him. Next thing in the morning they would be visiting the mountain top and icy caves.

CHAPTER 7: MYSTICAL WARS

They entered the dark icy caves. They lit a torch and saw a giant snake:

"Who dares enters my cave?!!" asked the snake They did not respond. When they turned to look around the cave, they saw a statue of a Giant. The huge snake didn't have particularly good eyesight, so they sneaked past the snake, and hid behind the frozen giant. The torches that they were holding were slowly melting the ice of the giant after a few minutes of hiding, the ice had turned into water, and the giant asked who had freed him (the giant)? US and they (Chaltas and his team) answered. The Giant picked them up and jumped out of the cave. The Giant saw a paper fly out of Chaltas's pocket he took it and read it (giants know how to read). The Giant couldn't talk well but he could say simple words like me, smash, me need food, me strong. So, the giant said. *"Me come wit you on da journey."*

And Chaltas agreed so the Giant carried them, and they traveled fast across the icy mountains, where they camped out for the night. The Giant slept in a cave and Chaltas placed a dozen of torches around him. The next morning Tau made a massive mace from some of the stalagmite's stalactites in the cave for the Giant and they continued the journey. They went into the marshes and the Giant helped them across the sticky water so that they won't sink.

The fearless team were still venturing.

They entered the kingdom of the **pixies and gnomes**. When they saw the pixies and gnomes, they realized they were in an awfully long war. They took separate ways to cover more space not knowing they will be in separate sides fighting in the war. Lexi and Ou and the giant went on one side and Tau and Chaltas on the other. The best friends were approached by gnomes that had pitchforks and shovels and magical scythes. They told the Chaltas and Tau that they were fighting against a horrible enemy. They did not want to take part in the war. So they disagreed. The gnomes quickly pinned them down and put them under a spell. This made them aggressive toward the pixies and even their friends. Chaltas and Tau did not know that Lexi and Ou were in the pixies' team. The four friends were on opposite sides. The gnomes attacked first, the fairies followed, Lexi saw Chaltas and Chaltas saw Lexi, their *"teammates"* urged them to fight. Lexi shot arrows trying her best to avoid Chaltas. Chaltas played his flute a sleepy tune and about half of the fairies fell to the ground. Ou blasted the gnomes, and the Giant threw large boulders at the gnomes, Lexi and Chaltas came face to face Lexi shot a weak arrow at Chaltas so that the fairies thought that she was actually trying to hurt him. Chaltas dodged and punched at Lexi. The pixies were disgusted.

"Attack him said the fairies.

Lexi took Chaltas and Ou took Tau. Ou managed to grab a shiny apple off one of the enchanted trees that cures the rage spell. After Chaltas was cured, he felt bad for trying to attack his team mates. Ou told Tau that this village had enchanted apples and if any of them had gotten one it will be a great help. Chaltas remembered he had picked a similar apple. He reached into his pocket and showed the apple to Ou. Ou said it was exactly the one that he was talking about. They were still at war and the fairies were being destroyed by the gnomes. Chaltas and Lexi did not want to go, so Ou used his invisible coat and sneaked out, brought back a special stand and some apples and leaves. He inserted the bottles into the weird stand, and pressed the apples on top of the stand, the juice entered all the five bottles. He had brewed potions of energy. He put the leaves where he put the apples and a liquid from the leaves entered the other bottles. The potions of energy will give you speed like lightning and strength like lions. The potions of regeneration will cure you against the toxin of the spiders and heal you from any illness. So, he put all the bottles in supply sack and put it on a horse. We will use this against the flame golem

CHAPTER 8: ON COURSE

The team travelled for days through forests, deserts, and swamps. Eventually they reached the flame kingdom. When they got to the flame kingdom, they saw guards in front of the kingdom's gate. What are you here for? Asked both of the guardsmen standing in front of the gate. We are here to get a hut for a few days, Ou lied.

And between those hours they would incite a great battle, as Ou and his team had planned. They went through all the stores getting swords, amour and food. They went to their borrowed hut and started making plans. Tau worked on the swords. Lexi trained with her bow. Chaltas helped Ou with the plan and the giant was sharpening spikes to put on his club. Ou told Chaltas he had to train on telekinesis. Chaltas had to unlock that power from the flute. Chaltas tried to do it without playing the flute, but it did not work. He told Lexi to shoot an arrow at him; as soon as Lexi shot the arrow at him, he played the flute and it stopped right before it hit him, he several times.

He could not do it without the flute, then Ou took one spike from the giant's club and threw it at Chaltas. Chaltas did not have his flute; Lexi took it away. He put his hand in front of his head and the metal spike stopped and dropped onto the floor. Chaltas had not mastered it yet but that was a good start. Chaltas could stop things from hitting him and his friends. He could create an invisible defense, but he could not lift things not even a stick!

Ou devised a plan to help them destroy all the defenses and get close to the golem to defeat it. Chaltas stopped training on the telekinesis and rested for the night. A few hours later he got up and trained again; he tried for minutes and hours but he just could not lift anything up! He stopped and went to sit by a river to concentrate as the flow of water was his favourite sound. He played his flute and suddenly

out of nowhere a large clam came and gave Chaltas a magic orb, which shone.

It shined meaning it was no ordinary pearl The clam told Chaltas that this could help him teleport

anywhere he threw it the clam went back into the water and kept on bringing the magic orbs. Chaltas

got enough orbs for his team. He kept on training trying to levitate one small thing at a time. He could

now lift rocks but not boulders and no matter how hard he tried he just could not do it. Clearly noticing

Chaltas's frustration Ou came out to help. The key is to harness inner emotion and get it to do what

you please, but your emotions are scattered, and you cannot focus. Ou could get Chaltas to reorganize

his emotions by teaching him special incantations that come with a cost. Chaltas immediately wanted

to know what would happen when he uses the incantation. Ou said the incantations bring incredible

concentration and power at the cost of extreme weakness and maybe death. Chaltas was not

ready to lose his newfound powers or die. It was too much on his mind right now so he said

to Ou that he will think about it. Later in the night he woke up and saw a mob of guards

approaching so he woke his friends up and showed them the orbs he threw one of them to

proof what they can do. He threw it to a short distance and as the clam had said he instantly

teleported there. He run back and gave a few to his friends, and told them to keep it for the battle. They all suited up and got ready to fight the mob of guards. They defeated the mob who attacked them, and sneaked past the rest of the guardsmen and entered the market. They hid behind the stands and started the next phase of the plan. Lexi went to the flame palace and hid there. Chaltas dressed up in armour, and disguised himself like one of the guardsmen and joined them. He followed one into the golem throne room. He told both guards they were needed outside, and he was alone with the flame golem. Ou, still outside, brought up a wave from the river and drowned the remaining patrol guards. He told the giant he had to stay and when he heard them call, he will join them. Lexi took on one guard, defeated him, and just like Chaltas, disguised herself in the guard's armour. She went to guard the flame golem. Lexi and Chaltas were in the room. Ou could now sound the warning bell; all the guards came to see who sounded it. Ou wore his invisible cloak and sneaked past all the guards and entered the palace. He signalled the giant and the giant knocked through the castle walls, gathering every one's attention. Ou took out the guards and Chaltas and Lexi surrounded the flame golem. Was this it?!

CHAPTER 9: FIRE AND FURY

The flame golem blasted them, and they flew into the air. Lexi shot an arrow and it stuck to the wall she swung and kicked the flame golem. Even getting close to the flame golem was a problem; he was about a hundred of degrees hot. He melted Lexi's golden boots and she fell with a thud. Chaltas tried to slice through with a flame hand but this didn't do a thing. Water was their best option. The flame golem punched, and Chaltas blocked it with the psychic shield. Lexi attached a water bottle and shot it into one of the cracks of the flame golem. The flame golem knocked Lexi away and took Chaltas. He told him his great grandfather took the flute away from him and the only way he will not kill them is if he gives him the flute. He showed Chaltas his friends tied up all together even the giant. He was forced to do it as the flame soldiers brought their spears closer to his friends. He took the flute and gave it to the flame golem. Chaltas' friends looked relieved (What! Did they think he was going to give them in for the flute?) The golem crushed the flute and absorbed its power. He became larger and had all the powers that Chaltas had. He tore through the castle walls and walked. He melted everything that he touched. His guards were ordered to throw Lexi and her friends into the dungeon, and they did.

They stayed there for two days. Chaltas could not use his flame hand to slice through, but he could use one of those orbs. Ou's staff, Tau's spear, Lexi's crossbow they were taken away. And we all know what happened to Chaltas's flute. Out of nowhere a total stranger came and unlocked the doors for them.

Tau knew something about the stranger. They came out and retrieved their weapons except Chaltas. He took two swords and a shield from the box. He knocked two guards out with his hand. Ou set of the alarm intentionally and put ice all over the floor. Tau broke the path between the guards and them. They run towards the flame golem. The flame golem melted down all the houses that were on his way. He headed to the kingdom where Chaltas came from. He snuck behind the massive golem. The flame golem saw him and blew fire on him. Chaltas was just an ordinary person. But a voice said: "Chaltas, I am your great grandfather the god of wind (Oya).

Please insert Image #9 here. One of two images selected from this website https://www.gettyimages.com/ **as suggested by the Publisher. Creative #: 1410138386**

The voice said, blow into your palm. Chaltas followed the order and did it. Then the voice said shape it into anything you want. Chaltas shaped it into his flute and he played it. He got all his powers back. The voice turned into a whirlwind and descended into the nearby lake. Chaltas took some water from the lake and used his powers of the wind to splash it on the flame golem. The flame golem got up and brought flame gargoyles. Lexi told Chaltas they could handle it. Chaltas went after the flame golem. He flew up with the wind and he put his sword in some of the cracks in the flame golems skin. The golem was turning into rock; they needed more water. The giant could handle the gargoyles.

Chaltas flew up in the air and went after the golem. He was in the air and the golem batted him deep into the ground. Then Chaltas said the incantation and concentrated all his power on the golem. Tau furiously threw his spear at the golem. Ou threw water from the nearby river on the golem and Lexi shot all her arrows aiming into the cracks. The golem fell. He was defeated. They all rushed to Chaltas. Chaltas was fine but he was weak with no power left. They helped him up and got him some food and a place to rest.

CHAPTER 10: FOUND

Ice king was watching from his castle. His golems had been defeated. He knew Chaltas, and his friends would come after him. He prepared his armies and strengthened his defenses. However, he needed more power, and he knew he could get that from the ice elemental crystal. He stood from his tower and revealed something. He had an orb that could be used to see through people's mind and hear their thoughts. First he looked into Chaltas's mind. Chaltas was now training with weapons for the journey because he had lost his powers, yet he was determined to protect himself and his friends. Lexi was sharpening her arrows and getting ready to train with Chaltas, but she was thinking about all that she had come through together with her new friends, she wanted to stay but she was used to being alone and surviving. She also thought about all the near-death experiences she had on this journey. Ou was practicing spells and getting ready for the journey; also he noticed they had become better their weaknesses were weaker and their strengths stronger. Knowing what each one of them was doing or thinking, the King turned off his mystical orb.

Meanwhile, Chaltas was ready to face anything with his new friends. Tau was remembering that he was from the Vikings city, but he fled the city as a kid because of the wars, he could not wait to get there. His sister was captured during the war, so his parents told him to escape. He did. Ou was still examining the spear he found out that it could be charged up by elemental crystals. Ou showed his friends about his new findings. They had to get some of the elemental crystals to charge Tau's spear to full power. The Ice King also had to get some of the crystals to charge him up to full power, but to hold Chaltas and his team back, the King got bounty hunters to go after them. The team started on their journey to the Viking city, it took days, and they were running out of supplies so they used the last of their supplies to get to a nearby village. They entered the village and traded all of their remaining supplies to get a hut. Most of the villagers noticed them from the battle they had against the Moss golem and offered them gifts as they walked down the path to their hut.

Once they had reached, they planned on the next move to get to the Viking city. Ou knew the gems were in the mines so they had to sneak past the guards into the mine to get them. On their way out of the village Tau saw his spear was glowing, it's because we are getting closer to the gems. Ou said. Lexi took one look back and saw a figure running up to them, Lexi warned the others that a guy with a staff and axes was following them. Run. Said Chaltas as the hunter was running toward them, the hunter threw an axe at Tau, Chaltas forgot he had no power and he tried to block using his mind and just about the axe was about to hurt Chaltas and Tau, Tau's spear flew out of his hand and blocked. As they run, they noticed that someone had let their horses off the stable. As the hunter got closer Lexi shot and arrow at him, but he dodged it. They run to the horses, mounted and rode away very quickly. Who was he? Tau asked. He might be a bounty hunter. Ou answered. They had no place to rest so they kept on riding. In the middle of the night, they stopped on a shore and rested on the sand. Next, they rode to village where they all got supplies from the villagers. The next few days nothing happened, they rode towards the Ice kingdom. The bounty hunter was still on their back they had to be always ready. One time during the day when having a meal, the bounty hunter showed up, they all got their weapons ready. The bounty hunter charged at them with his axes. Chaltas blocked with his sword. Lexi shot an arrow at him, and Ou blasted him with a fireball. Tau launched his spear at the bounty hunter. Chaltas distracted the hunter also the weapons could hit him. They did hit him. They had gotten rid of one of the hunters but they need to be prepared in case they were more. . They were close to the Ice kingdom; it was getting cold. They had prepared and had gotten the right clothing for the weather. Lexi was still considering leaving because it was too dangerous. Chaltas warned them as they walked towards the golem. The golem was asleep, they had to be quiet. Lexi shot and arrow with a rope attached, and they climbed on to one of the ice spikes to get a better view. They saw the Ice King, standing in his tower with Chaltas' mom, he wanted to rush in and get his mom as quickly as he could, but they had to be sneaky, so they don't wake up the golem. The ice king saw them, and quickly called his guards. He also summoned the golem from its long rest and told it to destroy Chaltas and his team and also bring him Tau's spear. The golem obeyed. This golem was more powerful than any of the other golems they had battled before because it has absorbed all the power from the previous golems when they died. The ice golem shot glaciers of ice at the team through its mouth. Lexi and Ou shot their projectiles at the glaciers to stop them from hitting them, Chaltas run up one up the glaciers and tried to hit the golem with his sword, the golem saw him coming and batted him away with his hand. Chaltas fell but he wasn't hurt, he stuck the landing. Tau threw his spear at the golem in attempt to deform the golem, Lexi shot three arrows at the golem all three hitting but doing truly little damage. Ou launched another few fireballs and seeing it was not effective he tried something different. Lexi attached some of the dynamite she got some time ago to her arrows and hoping upon impact it will explode. It did the golem was dizzy and Ou and Tau and Chaltas could strike one critical hit. Chaltas run on one of the fireballs

Ou blasted and jumped of it right before impact. He dug the sword deep into the chest of the ice golem. Tau's spear also impaled the golem. Lexi shot a few more dynamite arrows as she was cautious not to miss because she only had a few left and she didn't want to hit her friends. The golem was confused and weak, the Ice King came down from his tower and added chunks and pieces of the other golems to the ice golem, now it had magma and mossy rock around it. It spewed lava out of his hand and rained rocks and glaciers from its mouth. Lexi had one more dynamite arrow left and she needed the explosion to be much bigger so she added all the dynamite and tied it onto the arrow. Chaltas distracted the beast by slicing and making marks in its leg. Ou made a massive fireball which drained a lot of his energy and Tau threw his spear which was attached with the mega dynamite arrow into the golems mouth it exploded giving them time to find his mom. They entered the castle and saw guards filling the halls they all rushed into the Castle. Lexi shot some arrows at the guards and Chaltas took some of them out with his sword. Tau impaled a few guards and Ou fire-balled the rest of them. They stormed into the castle and saw the Ice King right there. Where is my mom? Chaltas asked. He was ignored; instead the King summoned more golems but this time they were human sized. Chaltas and Tau took on the large golem and Lexi and Ou took on the golems. The ice golem took out his staff and launched exploding snowballs at Chaltas and Tau. They dodged but the fire and destruction was below them they charged at him. Chaltas slashed his sword towards his face but the golem dodged he had enough time to get Tau's spear. Lexi and Ou were done with the golems and they came to help. As they were battling, and the ice golem was distracted. Chaltas was filled with the raw energy from Tau's spear and he pushed all the power into his sword and they all struck the final hit. They had defeated the golem. They went up the tower to get Chaltas mom. Mom! Chaltas cried with joy as he hugged her. The team was ready to go home. On the journey home Chaltas' mom told the team that it was not the last of the Ice King. As they went back to their Kingdom and were crowned protectors, they knew the Ice King could attack at anytime, and so they were ever prepared. As these Fearless Four protected their Kingdom for decades, they became known in neighboring Kingdoms as they fearsome warriors.

END

Printed in the United States
by Baker & Taylor Publisher Services